W9-AVI-453

JOE BOAT

By Sandy Riggs
Illustrated by Kristin Barr

BARRON'S

Table of Contents

Illustrations on pages 21 and 23 created by Carol Stutz

All inquiries should be addressed to:
Barron's Educational Series, Inc.
250 Wireless Boulevard
Hauppauge, New York 11788
www.barronseduc.com

Library of Congress Catalog Card No.: 2005054187

ISBN-13: 978-0-7641-3296-4
ISBN-10: 0-7641-3296-2

Library of Congress Cataloging-in-Publication Data
Riggs, Sandy, 1940–
    Joe Boat / Sandy Riggs.
        p. cm. – (Reader's clubhouse)
        Summary: Joe the tugboat dreams of traveling around the world, but when anoth-
er boat asks for his help, he realizes he is needed and his voyage can wait for another
day. Includes facts about boats, a related activity, and word list.
        ISBN-13: 978-0-7641-3296-4
        ISBN-10: 0-7641-3296-2
        (1. Tugboats—Fiction. 2. Boats and boating—Fiction. 3. Responsibility—Fiction.
4. Voyages around the world—Fiction.) I. Title. II. Series.

PZ7.R44247Jo 2006
(E)—dc22

                                                                                                2005054187

Date of manufacture: 09/2009
Manufactured by: Kwong Fat Offset Printing Co., Ltd.
                    Dongguan City, China

PRINTED IN CHINA
9 8 7 6 5 4

Dear Parent and Educator,

Welcome to the Barron's Reader's Clubhouse, a series of books that provide a phonics approach to reading.

Phonics is the relationship between letters and sounds. It is a system that teaches children that letters have specific sounds. Level 1 books introduce the short-vowel sounds. Level 2 books progress to the long-vowel sounds. This progression matches how phonics is taught in many classrooms.

Joe Boat introduces the long "o" sound. Simple words with this long-vowel sound are called **decodable words.** The child knows how to sound out these words because he or she has learned the sound they include. This story also contains **high-frequency words.** These are common, everyday words that the child learns to read by sight. High-frequency words help ensure fluency and comprehension. **Challenging words** go a little beyond the reading level. The child will identify these words with help from the illustration on the page. All words are listed by their category on page 24.

Here are some coaching and prompting statements you can use to help a young reader read *Joe Boat*:

- **On page 4, "Joe" is a decodable word. Point to the word and say:**

   Read this word. How did you sound the word out? What sounds did it make?

   Note: There are many opportunities to repeat the above instruction throughout the book.

- **On page 7, "float" is a challenging word. Point to the word and say:**

   Read this word. It rhymes with "boat." How did you know the word? Did you look at the picture? How did it help?

You'll find more coaching ideas on the Reader's Clubhouse Web site: *www.barronsclubhouse.com.* Reader's Clubhouse is designed to teach and reinforce reading skills in a fun way. We hope you enjoy helping children discover their love of reading!

Sincerely,

Nancy Harris

Nancy Harris
Reading Consultant

Joe is a little boat.

He has big hopes.

Joe would like to go to sea.

Joe would float away
from home.

He would go around
the globe.

Where would Joe go?

He would go to Rome.

He would go to Nome.

"Wake up, Joe," a big boat
yells. "I need you."

Joe helps the boat. It has a
load of coal. The big boat
says, "Thank you, Joe."

Then Joe sees smoke.
He moves fast.

Joe puts foam on the fire.
The big boat is safe.

The big boat says,
"Thank you, Joe. You did
a good job!"

Joe always does a good job. All the boats tell him so.

Joe still wants to roam
the sea.

But for now, Joe will
stay home.

Fun Facts About
Boats

- The oldest seagoing ship is the *Star of India,* which was built in 1863!

- The world's smallest submarine is the *Water Beetle,* which is 116 inches (295 centimeters) long. That's about half as long as a car.

- There are many different types of boats. Some boats are powered by wind and sails, and others are powered by motors. Some carry passengers, some tow large ships, some transport cargo. Some boats are even used as homes for entire families.

  Look at the boats on the next page. Do you know what each boat is used for?

tugboat

sailboat

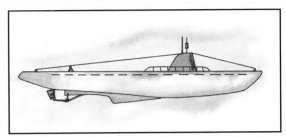

submarine

cargo ship

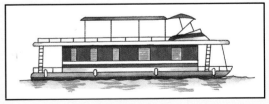

houseboat

Build a Sailboat

You will need:

- wide plastic lid (like the lid from a margarine tub)
- drinking straw
- construction paper
- safety scissors
- hole punch
- small ball of modeling clay or play dough
- crayons, markers, and/or stickers

1. Cut a triangle from a piece of construction paper to use as your sail. Decorate the sail with crayons, markers, and/or stickers.

2. Punch three holes along one side of the triangle.

3. Weave a drinking straw (the boat's mast) through the holes in the sail.

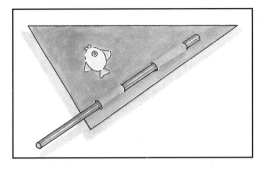

4. Put a small ball of clay on the inside of the plastic lid. Push the end of the drinking straw into the clay.

You now have a little sailboat that can actually float in water!

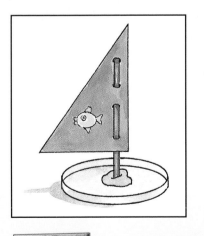

Word List

Challenging Words	float		
Long O Decodable Words	boat boats coal foam globe home hopes Joe load	Nome roam Rome smoke	
High-Frequency Words	a all always around away big but did does for from go good has	he helps him I is it like little moves now of on puts says	sees so thank the then to up wants where would you